I Have Another Language
The Language Is Dance

Eleanor Schick

MACMILLAN PUBLISHING COMPANY   NEW YORK

Maxwell Macmillan Canada   Toronto

Maxwell Macmillan International
New York   Oxford   Singapore   Sydney

Macmillan Publishing Company is part of the Maxwell Communication Group of Companies.

Macmillan Publishing Company
866 Third Avenue
New York, NY 10022

Maxwell Macmillan Canada, Inc.
1200 Eglinton Avenue East
Suite 200
Don Mills, Ontario M3C 3N1

First edition
Printed in the United States of America
1 3 5 7 9 10 8 6 4 2
The text of this book is set in 18 pt. ITC Usherwood Book.
The illustrations are rendered in pencil.
Library of Congress Cataloging-in-Publication Data
Schick, Eleanor.
I have another language : the language is dance / written and illustrated by Eleanor Schick.
— 1st ed.
p.   cm.
Summary: A young girl expresses her joy in the act of dancing.
ISBN 0-02-781209-X
[1. Dancing—Fiction.]   I. Title.
PZ7.S3445Iaf   1992   [Fic]—dc20   91-9485

For Sierra Niccole

It's morning. I'm still feeling the dream I had last night, but I can't say it in words. I'm ready for school. It's a special day. It feels like everything I do is for the first time.

In school, the breeze blowing through the window smells of spring, even though it's winter.

And a red-blossomed begonia
has opened in the sun.

I come to dance class early,
to stretch in the quiet of the room.

My body quivers,
thinking of tonight.

The class begins.
I exercise hard,

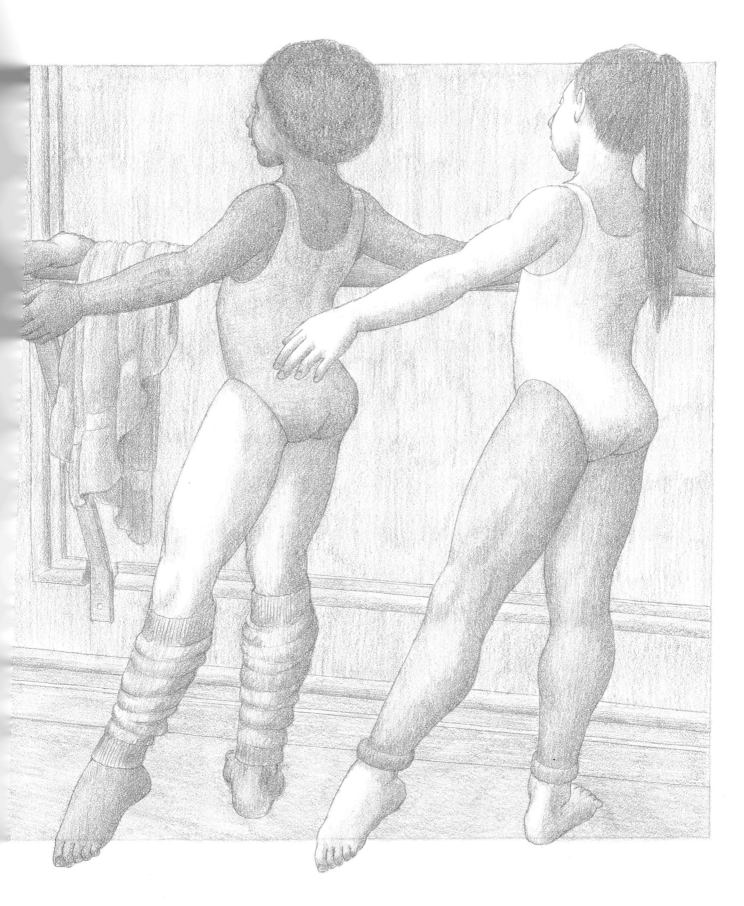

till sweat streams down
my face and back.

Music fills the room. We
do our leaps across the floor.

We want to dance full out, but our
teacher tells us, "Save it for tonight."

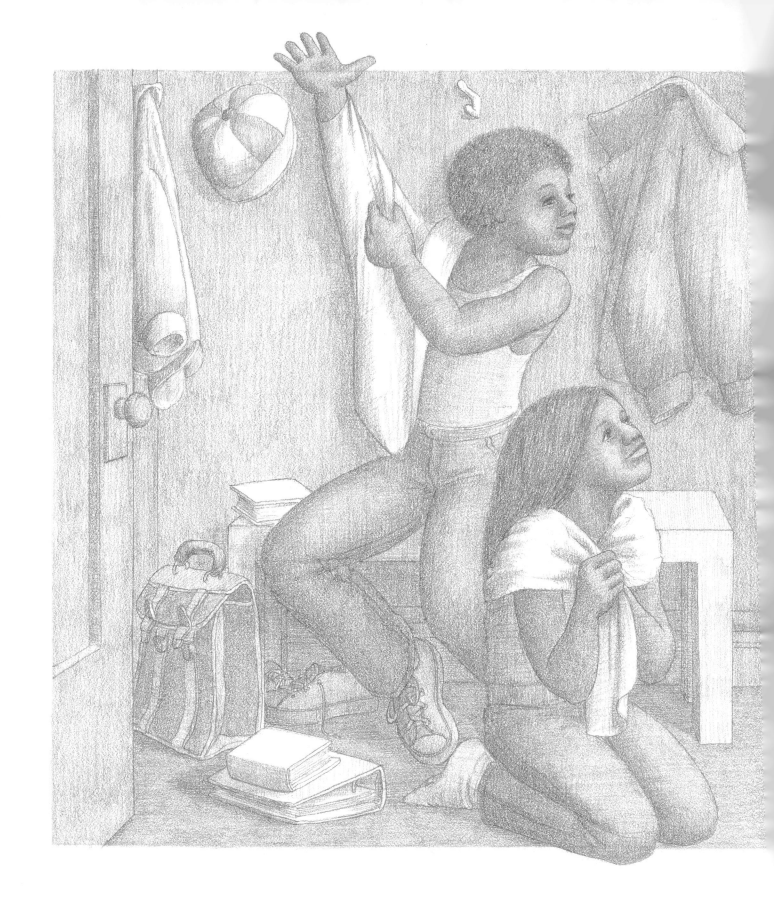

Now we'll go home
to rest

and prepare,
because

tonight, there is
a performance.

I've never danced
on a stage

in a theater
before.

I've never worn
makeup.

I can feel how
exciting it all is.

We take our places on stage.
The audience is suddenly still.
The curtain rises. The music begins.

Under the lights, as I
dance, every movement feels
more real than it ever has before.

I can feel the bright red of that flower,
and the smell of spring in the wind.

Inside the music, my body
remembers last night's dream.

Things I can't say in words
run through my body as I dance.

I feel them again,
in a new way.

When our performance ends, the people in
the audience clap and rise to their feet.
We know they have felt our feelings. Their
applause wraps around us all, like a hug.

We feel wonderful.
Our performance was
everything we hoped
it would be, and more!

Because we feel the power
of speaking another language:
the language of dance.

At night, when I hug Mama, she
cries from happiness, saying how
beautiful it all was.

I close my eyes. The smell of roses
fills my room. Feelings run through
me that words can't say, and that's
all right because I have a way to say
them. Tomorrow I will dance again!